Joseph's Cradle

Jude Daly

Otter-Barry BOOKS

In the heart of the village stood a magnificent, ancient tree.

Year after year, grown-ups gathered in its shade and children climbed up into its branches – to play or to eat its juicy fruit before the birds did.

One child, Joseph, even tried
climbing to the top of the tree.
And one day he really did reach
the top.

Afterwards, he practically
flew home, shouting, "Mama,
Mama, I touched the sky!"

The years went by.
Joseph grew up and married,
and the tree was always a
part of his life.

But just before his
wife, Mandisa, was due to
give birth to their first child,
a sudden wind whipped
through the village, ripping
the old tree out of the ground
as if it was a matchstick.

The shocked villagers gathered around the gaping hole. They listened as one man told the story of how Joseph climbed to the top of the tree and touched the sky.

"Haai!" said Joseph. "Now my baby will never be able to do that!"

The old tree was chopped up for firewood and shared out.
But Joseph chose instead a solid piece of its trunk.

Scoop-scoop went the men's shovels as they filled in
the hole. But suddenly Joseph yelled, "Whoah!"

Then he dashed home.

But in no time he was back with a young tree
that he had grown from seed.

Carefully he planted it where the old tree had stood.

Each morning Joseph
watered the little tree,
dreaming of it with
grown-ups sheltering
in its shade and with
children and birds in its
branches.

Each evening he carved
his piece of the old
tree's trunk.

"What are you making,
Joseph?" Mandisa asked.

But Joseph simply
smiled and said,
"Wait and see!"

So Mandisa waited…

and soon a shape emerged – **a cradle**.

When baby Sisi was born, Joseph longed to tell the whole world about his sweet, beautiful daughter.

That night, and every night, he sat beside the cradle and rocked Sisi to an African lullaby:

"Thula thul,
Thula baba,
Thula sana."

Soon Sisi outgrew the cradle. But Joseph lovingly carved her name into its side.

Then he passed the cradle to his neighbour, whose baby was due soon.

And so a tradition began.
Each new baby in the village slept in
Joseph's cradle until they outgrew it,
and then Joseph carved the baby's name
into the cradle's side.

By the time Sisi was married, with children of her own, Joseph's dream had come true.

The little tree he had planted before Sisi was born was now a big tree, with grown-ups in its shade and children, including his grandchildren, in its branches.

Then, one terrible day, when Sisi's children were all grown up, a raging fire swept through the veld. It roared and burned, and in no time it was just outside the village.

Joseph and Mandisa, with all the other elders and children, were taken over the hill to the safety of another village. Everyone else stayed behind and bravely fought the flames.

All the houses were saved except for one.... Joseph's and Mandisa's house was burnt to the ground, with everything inside it.

The men soon set about building Joseph and Mandisa a new home.
Meanwhile Sisi searched for Joseph's cradle. Fearing it had been
destroyed in the fire, she wept to think that her first grandchild, due by
the next full moon, would never sleep in the beautiful cradle.

But over the hills, Joseph
was busy!

He spent his days waxing and
polishing the cradle. Then he
wrapped it in a sheepskin,
ready for the journey home.

At last it was time for the elders and children to return. And when the villagers saw them coming over the hill, they broke into song.

But when Joseph saw his new house, the whole village fell silent to watch an old man dance like a young gazelle.

That night, Joseph and Mandisa sat outside their brand-new house.
An almost full moon rose above the big tree that stood in the heart
of the village.

Sisi came to join them, and that's when she saw it...
Joseph's cradle.

This time it was Sisi who danced for joy!
Soon her grandchild would be rocked to sleep in her father's
beautiful wooden cradle, soothed by an African lullaby:
  "*Thula thul,*
      Thula baba,
          Thula sana."

About the story

Reg Evans was an English actor who moved to Australia in the 1950s.
Also a craftsman, he carved a wooden cradle for a friend's new baby.
The cradle was then passed on, and on, so that each new baby in the community
of St Andrews, Victoria, could spend at least one night in it and have
their name carved on the cradle.

Tragically, Reg died in the Victorian Bushfires of 2009.
It was feared that the cradle had also been destroyed.
But a local man who had slept in it as an infant had taken the cradle to Canberra,
where he was now living, so that his newborn daughter could sleep in it.
And so the cradle survived and has since been returned to the community.

Stories, like people, travel. *Joseph's Cradle*, inspired by Reg Evans's story and with
the generous consent of his daughter, Claire, is set far away from Australia in a landscape
familiar to me - South Africa, home to the world heritage site, "The Cradle of Humankind".

Thula (pronounced Toola) *thul, thula baba, thula sana* is part of a traditional
Zulu lullaby that translates as *Hush, my child, hush, my baby*.

Jude Daly